# ALEX
## and
# ROY

## Mary Dickinson

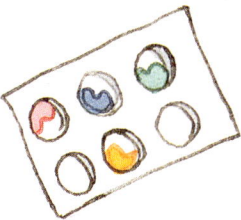

### Illustrated by
### Charlotte Firmin

**Hippo**

Scholastic Children's Books,
Scholastic Publications Ltd,
7-9 Pratt Street, London NW1 0AE, UK

Scholastic Inc.,
555 Broadway, New York, NY 10012-3999, USA

Scholastic Canada Ltd,
123 Newkirk Road, Richmond Hill,
Ontario, Canada L4C 3G5

Ashton Scholastic Pty Ltd,
PO Box 579, Gosford, New South Wales,
Australia

Ashton Scholastic Ltd,
Private Bag 92801, Penrose, Auckland,
New Zealand

First published in hardback by André Deutsch Ltd, 1981
Published by Scholastic Publications Ltd, 1983
Reissued by Scholastic Publications Ltd, 1995

Text copyright © Mary Dickinson, 1981
Illustrations copyright © Charlotte Firmin, 1981

ISBN: 0 590 13172 9

Typeset by Rapid Reprographics
Printed in Belgium by Proost International

All rights reserved

10 9 8 7 6 5 4 3 2 1

Mary Dickinson and Charlotte Firmin have asserted their moral right to be identified
as the author and illustrator of the work respectively, in accordance with the
Copyright, Designs and Patents Act 1988.

Brrring brrring, went the doorbell.

"Oh good," said Alex's mother. "That's Roy come to play."
"It's not good," said Alex. "I don't want to play with Roy."
And he stomped off into his bedroom.

Alex's mother opened the door.
It was Roy with his big sister Renee.
"Sorry I can't stop," said Renee. "Dad's waiting in the car. I don't want to be late at the hairdresser's."
"Come in, Roy," said Alex's mother. "Alex will be here in a minute."
She said it very loudly, hoping Alex would hear. But no Alex appeared.

"Where is Alex?" asked Roy.

"I think he's in his room," said Alex's mother. "Let's have a look."

Together they peered into Alex's room.

Alex was sitting behind the door, looking very, very, very cross.

Only his mother saw him.

She thought it best not to disturb him.

"I'm sure Alex will come out in a minute," she told Roy. "Could you help me while you're waiting?"

"Oh yes," said Roy. "I'm good at helping."

On the kitchen floor there were two boxes
full of shopping.
"Could you put the shopping away, please?"
asked Alex's mother.
"Yes," said Roy. "I'm good at putting
things away."

Roy worked very hard at putting the shopping away. Alex's mother noticed an eye at the kitchen door. But she said nothing.

When Roy had finished, he pushed the empty boxes
together and sat himself inside one.
"Brrrum, brum brum," he said. "Look at my car.
It's got a back and a front."
"That's a good idea," said Alex's mother.
"All you need now is a passenger." She could
see a head peeping round the kitchen door,
but she still said nothing.

Suddenly Alex strolled into the kitchen.
"Can I have a go?" he asked Roy.
"I'm the driver," said Roy. "There's room
for you in the back. Where do you want to go?"
Alex thought a little. "To the station,
please. I've a train to catch."

They drove as fast as they could go, but they had to stop because some men were mending the road. Alex missed his train.

They went to visit Alex's granny. They took her a can of coke. She gave them presents, just as she always did.

They went to see what Renee was doing at the hairdresser's. They saw some very strange sights.

They drove all the way to Africa; but they only saw two lions.

They drove for miles and miles and miles.
When they couldn't think of anywhere
else to go, they painted their car red,
with a yellow stripe along one side.

Just as they had finished, the doorbell rang.

"That'll be Renee," said Alex's mother. "Time for Roy to go home."

"Can't he stay for lunch?" asked Alex.

"Ooh, Alex," said his mother crossly. "You change your mind more times than you change your socks! At first you didn't want Roy to come. Now you don't want him to go. I'm sorry, Roy, I haven't cooked enough for you to stay, but you can stay another day."

Alex's mother let Renee in.
She had had her hair cut very short.
It made Alex and Roy giggle.
Alex's mother said nothing. She wasn't
sure if she liked Renee's new hairstyle.

Roy was sad to go home.
Alex said he could have one of the
boxes.
Roy left wearing it on his head, looking
out of a hole in the side.

Alex was sad, too.
Until he noticed that he could now be
the driver.
But he hadn't driven very far before his
mother waved for him to stop.
"Lunchtime!" she said.
"At last!" sighed Alex.